KU-712-143

ENGIE BENJY

Jollop to the Rescue

Adapted from the original episode by Bridget Appleby

Dan

Jollop

Engie Benjy

Farmer Fred had just made a delivery to Engie Benjy's garage.

"Look, team!" said Engie Benjy. "Orange Custard Fizz for breakfast!"

"**UGH!**" grumbled Jollop.

"I know it's not your favourite, Jollop, but your little cousin Jelly is coming to stay, and she loves it! You remember Jelly, don't you?"

Dan found a picture of Jelly in his compartment, and held it up.

"Such a sweet little dog," said Engie.

"**UGH!**" growled Jollop. Jollop didn't like cousin Jelly.

When Jelly arrived, she gave Jollop a big Hello lick. "**YUCK!**" thought Jollop.

Dan gave her a nice,
soft cushion to sleep on.

Jollop wasn't happy.

Jelly was very helpful.
She found the Orange
Custard Fizz which Jollop
had hidden. She brought Engie Benjy his porridge
and chocolate sandwich.

Jollop wasn't happy at all.

Suddenly, Plane's picture started flashing on the
alarm board! **"SOMETHING'S WRONG
WITH PLANE!"** cried Engie.

Outside, Plane flew down, and landed with a big **"HIC!"**

Pilot Pete shot out.

"What's wrong with Plane?" asked Engie.

"She's got the... Hiccups!" Pete sobbed.

Engie thought. "Hmmm... That is a problem!

WHADDA-WE-DO, DAN?"

Dan the Van handed him the useful 'What to do when Plane gets Hiccups' book, and Engie read, "If your Plane has hiccups, give it a drink..."

Jelly was listening carefully, and raced off to give Plane a big drink of Orange Custard Fizz.

But Engie hadn't finished reading,

" ... a drink of **ANYTHING** but Orange Custard Fizz! That makes a Plane spin and whizz!

OH NO, JELLY!"

Too late! Plane spun round and round and whizzed off, alone!

In a flash, Jollop chased after Plane as he took off.

"JOLLOP!
COME BACK!"

shouted Engie Benjy.

"Come on, everyone!
Let's follow them!"

Engie, Pilot Pete and Jelly all jumped into Dan,
and they raced off after Plane and Jollop.

Engie Benjy was worried.

"Jollop doesn't know how to fly a Plane," he said.

"We've got to get them down, **QUICKLY**!

Oh, if only Jollop could hear us!"

Dan pointed to Pilot Pete's pocket, where he kept his little plane-shaped walkie-talkie radio.

"You can borrow my walkie-talkie radio, Engie Benjy," said Pilot Pete,

"I use it to say good-night to Plane when I'm in bed. Jollop can hear you if you talk into it."

"Good idea, Pete," said Engie.

He switched it on.

"Jollop, **BARK** if you can hear me!"

Jollop's bark came out of the speaker on the little plane.

"Well done, Jollop! Now, Pete's going to tell you how to fly Plane!"

"Oh! I... I've never taught a dog to fly before," said Pete, sounding worried.

"Well, there's always a first time," Engie told him.

"You can do it!"

Pete took the walkie-talkie from Engie.

"Jollop?" he said, "Can you see the joystick? It looks a bit like a bone. Push it with your paw and use it to fly Plane!"

Jollop pushed the joystick and Plane began to turn around.

"HE'S DONE IT!" laughed Engie Benjy.

Back at the garage, Jelly put a line of dog biscuits on the ground to help Jollop find his way home.

"Look for the **BISCUITS**, Jollop!" shouted Engie.

Jollop licked his chops and looked down, but everyone watched anxiously as Plane flew

lower

and

lower....

Plane landed and followed the
line of biscuits back to the garage.
He stopped suddenly and Jollop
shot out of the cockpit into the air.

"I CAN'T LOOK!"
said Pilot Pete, hiding his eyes.

Quick as a flash, Jelly grabbed
her nice, soft cushion and put it under
Jollop as he fell, so he wasn't hurt at all!

Pilot Pete rushed over to Plane and gave him a big hug.

"Plane, listen, your hiccups have gone!"

Engie Benjy laughed.
"That must be the shock
of landing, Pete. The book
says that if a drink doesn't
work, a shock will usually
do the trick!"

Engie Benjy turned to Jollop,
"You did it, Jollop!
You saved Plane and
you've saved the day!"
"Well done" said Jelly and
gave Jollop a big lick.

VROOM
VROOM!